I0719288

If Lee Had Not Won Gettysburg

WINSTON CHURCHILL

Foreword by Gary Lee Hall

REPRINTED BY

Wake Forest, NC
www.scuppernongpress.com

If Lee Had Not Won Gettysburg
By Winston Churchill

Foreword by Gary Lee Hall

©2024 The Scuppernong Press

First Printing

The Scuppernong Press
PO Box 1724
Wake Forest, NC 27588
www.scuppernongpress.com

Cover and book design by Frank B. Powell, III

International Standard Book Number

ISBN 978-1-942806-61-5

Library of Congress Control Number: 2024934637

Contents

Suppose.

In 1935, acclaimed Southern writer William Faulkner
wrote a passage which can only be fully understood
(or more specifically felt) by Southerners. It related to the
third day of Gettysburg before Pickett's Charge and Petti-
grew's Charge towards Cemetery Ridge. Sadly, it is probably not as well known by some Southerners today, but it
is a grand part of their history. It is a part of their heritage
which can be reclaimed, should be reclaimed.

"It's all now you see ... "

"For every Southern boy fourteen years old, not once
but whenever he wants it, there is the instant when it's
still not yet two o'clock on that July afternoon in 1863,
the brigades are in position behind the rail fence, the guns
are laid and ready in the woods and the furled flags are
already loosened to break out and Pickett himself with
his long oiled ringlets and his hat in one hand probably
and his sword in the other looking up the hill waiting for
Longstreet to give the word and it's all in the balance, it
hasn't happened yet, it hasn't even begun yet, it not only
hasn't begun yet but there is still time for it not to begin

against that position and those circumstances which made more men than Garnett and Kemper and Armistead and Wilcox look grave yet it's going to begin, we all know that, we have come too far with too much at stake and that moment doesn't need even a fourteen-year-old boy to think …

This time. Maybe this time …"

— William Faulkner
Intruder in the Dust

Five years earlier in December 1930, Sir Winston Churchill, at age 56, wrote his version of what might have been, *If Lee Had Not Won the Battle of Gettysburg*. He started with the postulation that Lee had been successful at Gettysburg and proceeded from there.

Churchill, a great leader of his time, not only wrote history, but made a great deal of history himself. An English soldier, he fought in Africa, led forces in World War I, and arguably saved the world from destruction in World War II. Winston lived a full life before writing the article on this significant part of the War Between the States. A soldier in the British Empire, he had served in India, Sudan, and in the 2nd Boer War in South Africa. A train derailment resulted in his capture and imprisonment in Pretoria. Escaping from the POW camp, Churchill made

 If Lee Had Not Won Gettysburg

his way to freedom in a well-reported adventure. Key, if not always successful, involvement in World War I was also part of Churchill's impressive service.

This article was written between the World Wars of 1914 and 1940. This period was called his "Wilderness Years" 1929-1939. Although active in politics and opinion, Winston held no political office during his "Wilderness Years." Clementine, Winston's wife, once said this period was, "a blessing in disguise." Winston replied, "At the moment it seems very effectively disguised." It was a time during which he was able to reflect on the War of Southern Independence and suggest another outcome.

It is not surprising Winston wrote of Gettysburg and his rewrite of the outcome. Churchill was an admirer of the former British colony as he wrote his mother, "What an extraordinary people the Americans are." Obviously that admiration included the people of the South. In this article, one can sense his respect for General Robert E. Lee and the soldiers of the Confederacy.

Besides this article, readers will be entertained by the frequent, spiced, sharp, conversation between Churchill and Lady Astor (born in Danville, Virginia). Once Lady Astor told Churchill, "Winston, if I was married to you,

I would put poison in your tea." Winston without hesitation replied, "If you were my wife, I would drink it."

After completing this fictional, but admirable tale, Churchill was to lead Great Britain through the greatest threat the nation had ever experienced; Winston and the nation survived. His encouragement was sounded in his statement, "Never, never, never give up." Although there were many dark days during the war, the Allies continued on and, in the end, won. Serving as Prime Minister from 1940-1945, Churchill surprisingly lost his reelection in July 1945; from world hero to being voted out.

Someone interested in Churchill would be amiss not to look at the YouTube video "Marlborough scene from The Gathering Storm" *Britain Shall Prevail* (movie 2002). During this scene, Winston leaves his comrades behind and climbs alone up a hill to look down on the battlefield on the other side. In the empty fields below, the armies slowly form and engage in battle. Winston's ancestor, the 1st Duke of Marlborough, glances up from history to his descendant looking down from the hilltop in modern time. This was a look of understanding between the two historic figures; each fulfilling his duty in his time. No words were said, no words needed to be uttered.

                    If Lee Had Not Won Gettysburg

The Gathering Storm was the first book in Winston Churchill's volumes on World War II. Truer words could not be found to apply to that time in the mid Twentieth Century, throughout Winston's event filled life, and, of course, on 3 July 1861 on ridges in Pennsylvania.

The period between the World Wars, Winston sat at his desk to write his tale of a victorious Confederate States of America. He began with the fictional postulation General Lee had indeed been successful at Gettysburg which led to Southern Independence, an unusual approach. Winston carried it through 1914 and hinted of events in the upcoming 1940s.

A great historic hero, the study of Churchill's life is an important part of our history.

Here, enjoy Churchill's alternate history.

But suppose …

— Gary Lee Hall

In this speculative essay, first published in *Scribner's Magazine* in December, 1930, the distinguished statesman and historian assumes as a fact that Lee did triumph at Gettysburg and with skill and irony surveys the course of world history as it evolved after those momentous July days in 1863. This article is reprinted with the personal permission of the author.

General Robert E. Lee

If Lee Had Not Won Gettysburg

T HE quaint conceit of imagining what would have happened if some important or unimportant event had settled itself differently has become so fashionable that I am encouraged to enter upon an absurd speculation. What would have happened if Lee had not won the battle of Gettysburg? Once a great victory is won it dominates not only the future but the past. All the chains of consequence clink out as if they never could stop. The hopes that were shattered, the passions that were quelled, the sacrifices that were ineffectual are all swept out of the land of reality. Still, it may amuse an idle hour, and perhaps serve as a corrective to undue complacency, if at this moment in the twentieth century — so rich in assurance and prosperity, so calm and buoyant — we meditate for a spell upon the debt we owe to those Confederate soldiers who by a deathless feat of arms broke the Union front at Gettysburg and laid open a fair future to the world.

It always amuses historians and philosophers to pick out the tiny things, the sharp agate points, on which the ponderous balance of destiny turns; and certainly the details of the famous Confederate victory of Gettysburg furnish a fertile theme. There can be at this date no conceivable doubt that Pickett's charge would have been defeated if Stuart with his encircling cavalry had not arrived in the rear of the Union position at the supreme moment. Stuart might have been arrested in his decisive swoop if any one of twenty commonplace incidents had occurred. If, for instance, General Meade had organized his lines of communication with posts for defense against raids, or if he had used his cavalry to scout upon his flanks, he would have received timely warning. If General Warren had only thought of sending a battalion to hold Little Round Top, the rapid advance of the masses of Confederate cavalry must have been detected. If only President Davis's letter to General Lee, captured by Captain Dahlgren, revealing the Confederacy plans had reached Meade a few hours earlier, he might have escaped Lee's clutches.

Anything, we repeat, might have prevented Lee's magnificent combinations from synchronizing, and if so Pickett's repulse was sure. Gettysburg would have been a great Northern victory. It might have well been a final victory. Lee might indeed have made a successful retreat from the field. The Confederacy with its skilful generals and fierce armies, might have survived for another year, or even two, but once defeated decisively at Gettysburg, its doom was inevitable. The fall of Vicksburg, which happened only two days after Lee's immortal triumph, would in itself by opening the Mississippi to the river-fleets of the Union have cut the Secessionist States almost in half. Without wishing to dogmatize, we feel we are on solid ground in saying that the Southern States could not have survived the loss of a great battle in Pennsylvania, and the almost simultaneous bursting open of the Mississippi.

However, all went well. Once again by the narrowest of margins the compulsive pinch of military genius and soldierly valor produced a perfect result. The panic which engulfed the whole left of Meade's massive army has never been made a reproach against the Yankee troops. Every one knows they were stout fellows. But defeat is defeat, and rout is ruin. Three days only were required after the cannon at Gettysburg had ceased to thunder before General Lee fixed his headquarters in Washington. We need not here dwell upon the ludicrous features of the hurried flight to New York of all the politicians, place-hunters, contractors, sentimentalists and their retinues, which was so successfully accomplished. It is more agreeable to remember how Lincoln, "greatly falling with a falling State," preserved the poise and dignity of a nation. Never did his rugged yet sublime common sense render a finer service to his countrymen. He was never greater than in the hour of fatal defeat.

But of course there is no doubt whatever that the mere military victory which Lee gained at Gettysburg would not by itself have altered the history of the world. The loss of Washington would not have affected the immense numerical preponderance of the Union States. The advanced situation of their capital and its fall would have exposed them to a grave injury, would no doubt have considerably prolonged the war; but standing by itself this military episode, dazzling though it may be, could not have prevented the ultimate victory of the North. It is in the political sphere that we have to look to find the explanation of the triumphs begun upon the battlefield.

Curiously enough Lee furnishes an almost unique example of a regular and professional soldier who achieved the highest excellence both as a general and as a statesman. His ascendancy throughout the Confederate States on the morrow of his Gettysburg victory threw Jefferson Davis and his civil government irresistibly, indeed almost unconsciously, into the shade. The beloved and victorious commander arriving in the capital of his mighty antagonists found there the title-deeds which enabled him to pronounce the grand decrees of peace. Thus it happened that the guns of Gettysburg fired virtually the last shots in the American Civil War.

If Lee Had Not Won Gettysburg

President Jefferson Davis

THE movement of events then shifted to the other side of the Atlantic Ocean. England — the name by which the British Empire was then commonly described — had been riven morally in twain by the drama of the American struggle. We have always admired the steadfastness with which the Lancashire cotton operatives, though starved of cotton by the Northern blockade — our most prosperous county reduced to penury, almost become dependent upon the charity of the rest of England — nevertheless adhered to the Northern cause. The British working classes on the whole judged the quarrel through the eyes of Disraeli and rested solidly upon the side of the abolition of slavery. Indeed all Mr. Gladstone's democratic flair and noble eloquence would have failed, even upon the then restricted franchise, to carry England into the Confederate camp as a measure of policy. If Lee after his triumphal entry into Washington had merely been the soldier, his achievements would have ended on the battlefield. It was his august declaration that the victorious Confederacy would pursue no policy toward the African negroes which was not in harmony with the moral conceptions of western Europe that opened the highroads along which we are now marching so prosperously.

But even this famous gesture might have failed if it had not been caught up and implemented by the practical genius and trained parliamentary aptitudes of Gladstone.

If Lee Had Not Won Gettysburg

There is practically no doubt at this stage that the basic principle upon which the color question in the Southern States of America has been so happily settled owed its origin mainly to Gladstonian ingenuity and to the long statecraft of Britain in dealing with alien and more primitive populations. There was not only the need to declare the new fundamental relationship between master and servant, but the creation for the liberated slaves of institutions suited to their own cultural development and capable of affording them a different yet honorable status in a commonwealth, destined eventually to become almost world wide.

Let us only think what would have happened supposing the liberation of the slaves had been followed by some idiotic assertion of racial equality, and even by attempts to graft white democratic institutions upon the simple, docile, gifted African race belonging to a much earlier chapter in human history. We might have seen the whole of the Southern States invaded by gangs of carpetbagging politicians exploiting the ignorant and untutored colored vote against the white inhabitants and bringing the time-honored forms of parliamentary government into unmerited disrepute. We might have seen the sorry force of black legislators attempting to govern their former masters. Upon the rebound from this there must inevitably have been a strong reassertion of local white supremacy. By one device or another the franchises accorded to the negroes would have been taken from them. The constitutional principles of the Republic would have been proclaimed, only to be evaded or subverted; and many a warm-hearted philanthropist would have found his sojourn in the South no better than "A Fool's Errand."

But we must return to our main theme and to the procession of tremendous events which followed the Northern defeat at Gettysburg and the surrender of Washington. Lee's declaration abolishing slavery, coupled as it was with the inflexible resolve to secede from the American Union, opened the way for British intervention.

Within a month the formal treaty of alliance between the British Empire and the Confederacy had been signed. The terms of this alliance being both offensive and defensive revolutionized the military and naval situation. The Northern blockade could not be maintained even for a day in the face of the immense naval power of Britain. The opening of the Southern ports released the pent-up cotton, restored the finances, and replenished the arsenals of the Confederacy. The Northern forces at New Orleans were themselves immediately cut off and forced to capitulate. There could be no doubt of the power of the new allies to clear the Mississippi of Northern vessels throughout the whole of its course through the Confederate States. The prospect of a considerable British army embarking for Canada threatened the Union with a new military front.

                    If Lee Had Not Won Gettysburg

BUT none of these formidable events in the sphere of arms and material force would have daunted the resolution of President Lincoln, or weakened the fidelity of the Northern States and armies. It was Lee's declaration abolishing slavery which by a single master stroke gained the Confederacy an all-powerful ally, and spread a moral paralysis far and wide through the ranks of their enemies. The North were waging a war against Secession, but as the struggle had proceeded the moral issue of slavery had first sustained and then dominated the political quarrel. Now that the moral issue was withdrawn, now that the noble cause which inspired the Union armies and the governments behind them was gained, there was nothing left but a war of reconquest to be waged under circumstances infinitely more difficult and anxious than those which had already led to so much disappointment and defeat. Here was the South victorious, reinvigorated, reinforced, offering of her own free will to make a more complete abolition of the servile status on the American continent than even Lincoln had himself seen fit to demand. Was the war to continue against what soon must be heavy odds merely to assert the domination of one set of English-speaking people over another? Was blood to flow indefinitely in an ever-broadening stream to gratify national pride, or martial revenge ?

It was this deprivation of the moral issue which undermined the obduracy of the Northern States. Lincoln no longer rejected the Southern appeal for independence. "If," he declared in his famous speech in Madison Square Garden in New York, "our brothers in the South are willing faithfully to cleanse this continent of Negro slavery and if they will dwell beside us in neighborly good-will as an independent but friendly nation, it would not be right to prolong the slaughter on the question of sovereignty alone."

Thus peace came more swiftly than war had come. The Treaty of Harper's Ferry which was signed between the Union and Confederate States on the 6th of September, 1863, embodied the two fundamental propositions, that the South was independent, and the slaves were free. If the spirit of old John Brown had revisited the battle-scarred township which had been the scene of his life and death, it would have seen his cause victorious; but at a cost to the United States terrible indeed. Apart from the loss of blood and treasure, the American Union was riven in twain. Henceforth there would be two Americas in the same northern continent. One of them would have revived in a modern and embattled form its old ties of kinship and affiliation with the Mother Country across the ocean. It was evident, though peace might be signed and soldiers furl their flags, that profound antagonisms,

 If Lee Had Not Won Gettysburg

social, economic and military, underlay the life of the English-speaking world. Still slavery was abolished. As John Bright said: "At last, after the smoke of the battlefield has cleared away, the horrid shape which had cast its shadow over the whole continent had vanished and was gone forever."

A T this date, when all seems so simple and clear, one has hardly the patience to chronicle the bitter and lamentable developments which occupied the two succeeding generations.

But we may turn aside in our speculation to note how strangely the careers of Mr. Gladstone and Mr. Disraeli would have been altered if Lee had not won the battle of Gettysburg. Mr. Gladstone's threatened resignation from Lord Palmerston's Cabinet on the morrow of General Lee's pronouncement in favor of abolition induced a political crisis in England of the most intense character. Old friendships were severed, old rancors died, and new connections and resentments took their place. Lord Palmerston found himself at the parting of the ways. Having to choose between Mr. Gladstone and Lord John Russell, he did not hesitate. A Coalition Government was formed in which Lord Robert Cecil (afterward the great Lord Salisbury) became Foreign Secretary, but of which Mr. Gladstone was henceforward the driving force. We remember how he had said at Newcastle on October 7, 1862, "We know quite well that the people of the Northern States have not yet drunk of the cup — they will try hard to hold it far from their lips — which all the rest of the world see they nevertheless must drink. We may have our own ideas about slavery; we may be for or against the South; but there is no doubt that Jefferson Davis and the other soldiers of the South have made an army; they are making, it appears, a navy; and they have made what is more than either , they have made a nation." Now the slavery obstacle was out of the way and under the aegis of his aged chief, Lord Palmerston, who in Mr. Gladstone's words "desired the severance [of North and South] as the diminution of a dangerous power," and aided by the tempered incisiveness of Lord Robert Cecil, Mr. Gladstone achieved not merely the recognition but an abiding alliance between Great Britain and the Southern States. But this carried him far. In the main the friends of the Confederacy in England belonged to the aristocratic well-to-do and Tory classes of the nation; the democracy, as yet almost entirely unenfranchised, and most of the Liberal elements, sympathized with the North. Lord Palmerston's new government formed in September, 1863, although nominally Coalition, almost entirely embodied the elements of Tory strength and inspiration. No one can say that Gladstone's reunion with the Tories would have been

                    If Lee Had Not Won Gettysburg

William Ewart Gladstone, "greatest of Conservative
Empire and Commonwealth builders."

achieved apart from Gettysburg and Lee's declaration at Washington.

However, it was achieved, and henceforward the union of Mr. Gladstone and Lord Robert Cecil on all questions of Church, State, and Empire became an accomplished and fruitful fact. Once again the "rising hope of the stern and unbending Tories" had come back to his old friends, and the combination, armed as it was with prodigious executive success, reigned for a decade irresistible.

It is strange, musing on Mr. Gladstone's career, how easily he might have drifted into radical and democratic courses. How easily he might have persuaded himself that he, a Tory and authoritarian to his finger-tips, was fitted to be the popular, and even populist, leader of the working classes! There might in this event have stood to his credit nothing but sentimental pap, pusillanimous surrenders of British interests, and the easy and relaxing cosmopolitanism which would in practice have made him the friend of every country but his own. But the sabres of J.E.B. Stuart's cavalry and the bayonets of Pickett's division had, on the slopes of Gettysburg, embodied him forever in a revivified Tory party. His career thus became a harmony instead of a discord; and he holds his place in the series of great builders to whom the larger synthesis of the world is due.

 If Lee Had Not Won Gettysburg

Benjamin Disraeli, "idol of the toiling masses"

Precisely the reverse effect operated upon Mr. Disraeli. What had he to do with the Tory aristocracy? In his earlier days he was prejudiced in their eyes as a Jew by race. He had indeed only been saved from the stigma of exclusion from public life before the repeal of the Jewish disabilities by the fact of his having been baptized in infancy. He had stood originally for Parliament as a Radical. His natural place was with the left-out millions, with the dissenters, with the merchants of the North, with the voteless proletariat. He might never have found his place if Lee had not won the battle of Gettysburg. But for that he might have continued leading the Conservative party, educating them against their will, dragging them into all sorts of social policies which they resented, making them serve as agents for extensions of the franchise. Always indispensable, always distrusted, but for Lee and Gettysburg he might well have ended his life in the House of Lords with the exclamation "Power has come to me too late!"

But once he was united by the astonishing events of 1863 with the democratic and Radical forces of the nation, the real power of the man became apparent. He was in his native element. He had always espoused the cause of the North; and what he was pleased to describe as "the selfish and flagitious intrigue (of the Palmerston-Gladstone government) to split the American Union and to rebuild out of the miseries of a valiant nation the vanished

                    If Lee Had Not Won Gettysburg

empire of George III," aroused passions in England strong enough to cast him once and for all from Tory circles. He went where his instinct and nature led him, to the radical masses which were yearly gathering strength. It is to this we owe his immense contribution to our social services. If Disraeli had not been drawn out of the Conservative party, the whole of those great schemes of social and industrial insurance which are forever associated with his name, which followed so logically upon his speeches— "Health and the laws of health" ("*sanitas sanitatum omnia sanitas*") — might never have been passed into law in the nineteenth century. It might well have come about in the twentieth. It might have been left to sprout of the new democracy of some upstart from Scotland, Ireland, or even Wales, to give to England what her latest Socialist Prime Minister has described as "our incomparable social services." But "Dizzy," "The people's Dizzy," would never have set these merciful triumphs in his record.

We must return to the main theme. We may, however, note, by the way, that if Lee had not won the battle of Gettysburg, Gladstone would not have become the greatest of Conservative Empire and Commonwealth builders, nor would Disraeli have been the idol of the toiling masses. **Such is Fate.**

BUT we cannot occupy ourselves too long upon the fortunes of individuals. During the whole of the rest of the nineteenth century the United States of America, as the truncated Union continued to style itself, grew in wealth and population. An iron determination seemed to have taken hold of the entire people. By the eighties they were already cleared of their war debt, and indeed all traces of the war, except in the hearts of men, were entirely eradicated. But the hearts of men are strange things, and the hearts of nations are still stranger. Never could the American Union endure the ghastly amputation which had been forced upon it. Just as France after 1870 nursed for more than forty years her dream of revanche, so did the multiplying peoples of the American Union concentrate their thoughts upon another trial of arms.

And, to tell the truth, the behavior of the independent Confederacy helped but little in mitigating the ceaselessly fermenting wrath. The former Confederate States saw themselves possessed of a veteran army successful against numerous odds, and commanded by generals to whose military aptitude history has borne unquestioned tribute. To keep this army intact and — still more important — employed became a high problem of state. To the south of the Confederacy lay Mexico, in perennial alternation between anarchy and dictatorship. Lee's early experiences in the former Mexican war had familiarized him with the

                    If Lee Had Not Won Gettysburg

military aspects of the country and its problems, and we must admit that it was natural that he should wish to turn the bayonets of the Army of Northern Virginia upon this sporadically defended Eldorado. In spite of the pious protests of Mr. Disraeli's Liberal and pacifist government of 1884, the Confederate States after three years' sanguinary guerilla fighting conquered, subdued, and reorganized the vast territories of Mexico. These proceedings involved a continuous accretion of Southern military forces. At the close of the Mexican war, 700,000 trained and well-tried soldiers were marshalled under what the North still called "the rebel flag." In the face of these potentially menacing armaments, who can blame the Northern States for the precautions they took? Who can accuse them of provocation because they adopted the principle of compulsory military service? And when this was retorted by similar measures south of the Harper's Ferry Treaty line, can we be surprised that they increased the period of compulsory service from one year to two and thereby turned their multitudinous militia into the cadres of an army "second to none"? The Southern States, relying on their alliance with the supreme naval power of Britain, did not expend their money upon a salt-water navy. Their powerful iron-clad fleet was designed solely for the Mississippi. Nevertheless, on land and water the process of armament and counter-armament proceeded ceaselessly over the whole expanse of the North American continent. Immense fortresses guarded the frontiers on either side and sought to canalize the lines of reciprocal invasion. The wealth of the Union States enabled them at enormous sacrifice at once to fortify their southern front and to maintain a strong fleet and heavy military garrison in the fortified harbors of the great lakes of the Canadian frontier. By the nineties North America bristled with armaments of every kind, and what with the ceaseless growth of the Confederate army — in which the reconciled Negro population now formed a most important element — and the very large forces which England and Canada maintained in the North, it was computed that not less than 2,000,000 armed men with trained reserves of 6,000,000 were required to preserve the uneasy peace of the North American continent. Such a process could not go on without a climax of tragedy or remedy.

The climax which came in 1905 was perhaps induced by the agitation of war excitement arising from the Russo-Japanese conflict. The thunder of Asiatic cannon reverberated around the globe and everywhere found immense military organizations in an actively receptive state. Never has the atmosphere of the world been so loaded with explosive forces. Europe and North America were armed camps and a war of first magnitude was actually raging in Manchuria. At any moment, as the Dogger Bank incident had shown, the British Empire might be involved in war with Russia. Indeed we had been within the ace on that occasion. And apart from such accidents the British Treaty obligations toward Japan might automatically have drawn us in. The president of the United States had been formally advised by the powerful and highly competent American General Staff that the entry of Great Britain into such a war would offer in every way a favorable opportunity for settling once and for all with the Southern Republic. This fact was also obvious to most people. Thus at the same time throughout Europe and America precautionary measures of all kinds by land and sea were actively taken; and everywhere fleets and armies were assembled and arsenals clanged and flared by night and day.

NOW that these awful perils have been finally warded off, it seems to us almost incomprehensible they could have existed. Nevertheless, it is horrible even to reflect that scarcely a quarter of a century ago English-speaking people ranged on opposite sides, watched each other with ceaseless vigilance and drawn weapons. By the end of 1905 the tension was such that nothing could long avert a fratricidal struggle on a gigantic scale, except some great melting of hearts, some wave of inspiration which should lift the dull, deadly antagonisms of the hour to a level so high that — even as a mathematical quantity passing through infinity changes its sign — they would become actual unities.

We must not underrate the strength of the forces which on both sides of the Atlantic Ocean and on both sides of the American continental frontiers were laboring faithfully and dauntlessly to avert the hideous doom which kindred races seemed resolved to prepare for themselves. But these deep currents of sanity and goodwill would not have been effective unless the decisive moment had found simultaneously in England and the United States leaders great enough to dominate events and marvelously placed upon the summits of national power. In President Roosevelt and Mr. Arthur Balfour, the British Prime Minister, were present two diverse personalities which together embodied all the qualities necessary alike for profound negotiation and for supreme decision.

After all, when it happened it proved to be the easiest thing in the world. In fact it seemed as if it could not help happening, and we who look back upon it take it so much for granted that we can not understand how easily the most beneficent government of which human records are witness might have been replaced by the most horrible conflict and world tragedy.

The Balfour-Roosevelt negotiations had advanced some distance before President Wilson, the enlightened Virginian chief of the Southern Republic, was involved

                    If Lee Had Not Won Gettysburg

President Woodrow Wilson

in them. It must be remembered that whatever may be thought of Mr. Gladstone's cold-blooded coup in 1863, the policy of successive British governments had always been to assuage the antagonism between North and South. At every stage the British had sought to promote good-will and close association between her southern ally and the mighty northern power with whom she had so much in common. For instance, we should remember how in the Spanish-American War of 1898 the influence of Great Britain was used to the utmost and grave risks were run in order to limit the quarrel and to free the United States from any foreign menace. The restraining counsels of England on this occasion had led the Southern Republic to adopt a neutrality not only benevolent but actively helpful. Indeed in this war several veteran generals of the Confederate army had actually served as volunteers with the Union forces. So that one must understand that side by side with the piling up of armaments and the old antagonisms, there was an immense undertide of mutual liking and respect. It is the glory of Balfour-Roosevelt and Wilson — this august triumvirate — that they were able so to direct these tides that every opposing circumstance or element was swept before them.

On Christmas Day, 1905, was signed the Covenant of the English-speaking Association. The essence of this extraordinary measure was crystal clear. The doctrine of

   If Lee Had Not Won Gettysburg

common citizenship for all the peoples involved in the
agreement was proclaimed. There was not the slightest
interference with the existing arrangements of any member. All that happened was that henceforward the peoples
of the British Empire and of what were happily called in
the language of the line "The Re-United States" deemed
themselves to be members of one body and inheritors of
one estate. The flexibility of the plan which invaded no
national privacy, which left all particularisms entirely
unchallenged, which altered no institutions and required
no elaborate machinery, was its salvation. It was in fact
a moral and psychological rather than political reaction.
Hundreds of millions of people suddenly adopted a new
point of view. Without prejudice to their existing loyalties
and sentiments, they gave birth in themselves to a new
higher loyalty and a wider sentiment. The autumn of 1905
had seen the English-speaking world on the verge of ca-
tastrophe. The year did not die before they were associated
by indissoluble ties for the maintenance of peace between
themselves, for the prevention of war among outside powers, and for the economic development of their measure-
less resources and possessions.

The association had not been in existence for a decade before it was called upon to face an emergency not
less grave than that which had called it into being. Every one remembers the European crisis of August, 1914.

The murder of the Archduke at Sarajevo, the disruption or decay of the Austrian and Turkish Empires, the old quarrel between Germany and France and the increasing armaments of Russia — all taken together produced the most dangerous conjunction which Europe has ever known. Once the orders for Russian, Austrian, German, and French mobilization had been given and 12,000,000 soldiers were gathering upon the frontiers of their respective countries, it seemed nothing could avert a war which might well have become Armageddon itself.

What the course and consequences of such a war would have been are matters upon which we can only speculate. M. Bloch, in his thoughtful book published in 1909, indicated that such a war if fought with modern weapons would not be a short one. He predicted field operations would quickly degenerate into long lines of fortifications, and that a devastating stalemate with siege warfare, or trench warfare, lasting for years might well ensue. We know his opinions are not accepted by the leading military experts of most countries. But at any rate we can not doubt that a war in which four or five of the greatest European powers were engaged might well have led to the loss of many millions of lives, and to the destruction of capital that twenty years of toil, thrift, and privation could not have replaced. It is no exaggeration to say that had the crisis of general mobilization of August, 1914,

                                   If Lee Had Not Won Gettysburg

been followed by war, we might today in this island see income tax at four shillings or five shillings in the pound, and have one and a half million unemployed workmen on our hands. Even the United States, far across the ocean, might against all its traditions have been dragged into a purely European quarrel.

But in the nick of time friendly, though resolute, hands intervened to save Europe from what might well have been her ruin. It was inherent in the Covenant of the English-speaking Association that the ideal of mutual disarmament to the lowest point compatible with their joint safety should be adopted by the signatory members. It was also settled that every third year a conference of the whole association should be held in such places as might be found convenient. It happened that the third disarmament conference of the English-speaking Association — the E.S.A. as it is called for short — was actually in session in July, 1914. The association had found itself hampered in its policy of disarmament by the immense military and naval establishments maintained in Europe. Their plenipotentiaries were actually assembled to consider this problem when the infinitely graver issue burst upon them. They acted as men accustomed to deal with the greatest events. They felt so sure of themselves that they were able to run risks for others. On the 1st of August, when the German armies were already approaching the frontiers of Belgium, when the Austrian armies had actually begun the bombardment of Belgrade, and when all along the Russian and French borders desultory picket-firing had broken out, the E.S.A. tendered its friendly offices to all the mobilized powers, counselling them to halt their armies within ten miles of their own frontiers, and to seek a solution of their differences by peaceful discussion. The memorable document added "that failing a peaceful outcome the association must deem itself *ipso facto* at war with any power in either combination whose troops invaded the territory of its neighbor."

Although this suave yet menacing communication was received with indignation in many quarters, it in fact secured for Europe the breathing space which was so desperately required. The French had already forbidden their troops to approach within ten miles of the German frontier, and they replied in this sense. The Czar eagerly embraced the opportunity offered to him. The secret wishes of the Kaiser and his emotions at this juncture have necessarily been much disputed. There are those who allege that, carried away by the excitement of mobilization and the clang and clatter of moving armies, he was not disposed to halt his troops already on the threshold of the Duchy of Luxembourg. Others avow that he received the message with a scream of joy and fell exhausted into

                              If Lee Had Not Won Gettysburg

Kaiser Wilhelm

a chair exclaiming "Saved! Saved! Saved!" Whatever may have been the nature of the Imperial convulsion, all we know is that the acceptance of Germany was the last to reach the association. With its arrival, although there yet remained many weeks of anxious negotiation, the danger of a European war may be said to have passed away.

MOST of us have been so much absorbed by the immense increases of prosperity and wealth, or by the commercial activity and scientific and territorial development and exploitation which have been the history of the English-speaking world since 1905, that we have been inclined to allow European affairs to fall into a twilight of interest. Once the perils of 1914 had been successfully averted and the disarmament of Europe had been brought into harmony with that already effected by the E.S.A., the idea of "An United States of Europe" was bound to occur continually. The glittering spectacle of the great English-speaking combination, its assured safety, its boundless power, the rapidity with which wealth was created and widely distributed within its bounds, the sense of buoyancy and hope which seemed to pervade the entire population; all this pointed to European eyes a moral which none but the dullest could ignore. Whether the Emperor Wilhelm II will be successful in carrying the project of European unity forward by another important stage at the

   If Lee Had Not Won Gettysburg

forthcoming Pan-European Conference at Berlin in 1932,
is still a matter of prophecy. Should he achieve his pur-
pose he will have raised himself to a dazzling pinnacle of
fame and honor, and no one will be more pleased than the
members of the E.S.A. to witness the gradual formations
of another great area of tranquillity and co-operation like
that in which we ourselves have learned to dwell. If this
prize should fall to his Imperial Majesty, he may perhaps
reflect how easily his career might have been wrecked in
1914 by the outbreak of war, which might have cost him
his throne, and have laid his country in the dust. If today
he occupies in his old age the most splendid situation in
Europe, let him not forget that he might well have found
himself eating the bitter bread of exile, a dethroned sover-
eign, and a broken man loaded with unutterable reproach.

*And this, we repeat, might well have been his fate if
Lee had not won the battle of Gettysburg.*

Widely regarded as one of the greatest wartime leaders of the 20th century, Winston Churchill was born on November 30, 1874 at his family's ancestral home, Blenheim Palace in Oxfordshire. On his father's side, he was a member of the British aristocracy as a descendant of John Churchill, 1st Duke of Marlborough. His father, Lord Randolph Churchill, representing the Conservative Party, had been elected Member of Parliament for Woodstock in 1874. His mother, Jennie, was a daughter of Leonard Jerome, a wealthy New York financier and horse racing enthusiast.

Called the "The Last Lion," he was a legendary orator, a prolific writer, an earnest artist, and a long-term British statesman. Churchill twice served as prime minister of the United Kingdom, but is best remembered as the tenacious and forthright war leader who led his country against the seemingly unbeatable Nazis during World War II. By joining forces with both the United States and the Soviet Union, Churchill not only saved Britain but helped save all of Europe from the domination of Nazi Germany.

In 1908, Winston Churchill married Clementine Ogilvy Hozier after a short courtship. The couple had five children together: Diana, Randolph, Sarah, Marigold (who died as a toddler of tonsillitis) and Mary. They were married for 57 years

Churchill remained active. In 1946, he went on a lecture tour in the United States which included his very famous speech, "The Sinews of Peace," in which he warned of an "iron curtain" descending upon Europe. Churchill also continued to make speeches in the House of Commons and to relax at his home and paint.

Churchill also continued to write. He used this time to start his six-volume work, *The Second World War* (1948-1953).

During his later years, Churchill earned three impressive awards. On April 24, 1953, Churchill was made knight of the garter by Queen Elizabeth II, making him Sir Winston Churchill. Later the same year, Churchill was awarded the Nobel Prize in Literature, the only prime minister so honored. Ten years later, on April 9, 1963, President John F. Kennedy awarded Churchill with honorary U.S. citizenship, the first person to be so awarded.

Churchill died on January 24, 1965, at age 90 in his London home. He had remained a member of Parliament until a year before his death.

                    If Lee Had Not Won Gettysburg